FIND OUT
ABOUT
FOOD

BREAD AND CEREAL

by Tea Benduhn

Reading consultant: Susan Nations, M.Ed., author/literacy coach/
consultant in literacy development

WEEKLY READER®
PUBLISHING

Please visit our web site at: **www.garethstevens.com**
For a free color catalog describing our list of high-quality books,
call 1-800-542-2595 (USA) or 1-800-387-3178 (Canada).

Library of Congress Cataloging-in-Publication Data

Benduhn, Tea.
    Bread and cereal / Tea Benduhn.
        p. cm. — (Find out about food)
    Includes bibliographical references and index.
    ISBN: 978-0-8368-8250-6 (lib. bdg.)
    ISBN: 978-0-8368-8257-5 (softcover)
    1. Bread—Juvenile literature.   2. Grain—Juvenile literature.
  I. Title.
    TX769.B343   2007
    641.8'15—dc22   2007006045

This edition first published in 2008 by
Weekly Reader® Books
An imprint of Gareth Stevens Publishing
1 Reader's Digest Road
Pleasantville, NY 10570-7000 USA

Copyright © 2008 by Gareth Stevens, Inc.

Managing editor: Valerie J. Weber
Art direction: Tammy West
Graphic designer: Scott Krall
Picture research: Diane Laska-Swanke
Photographer: Gregg Andersen
Production: Jessica Yanke

Printed in the United States of America

1 2 3 4 5 6 7 8 9 11 10 09 08 07

Note to Educators and Parents

Reading is such an exciting adventure for young children! They are beginning to integrate their oral language skills with written language. To encourage children along the path to early literacy, books must be colorful, engaging, and interesting; they should invite the young reader to explore both the print and the pictures.

The *Find Out About Food* series is designed to help children understand the value of good nutrition and eating to stay healthy. In each book, young readers will learn how their favorite foods — and possibly some new ones — fit into a balanced diet.

Each book is specially designed to support the young reader in the reading process. The familiar topics are appealing to young children and invite them to read — and re-read — again and again. The full-color photographs and enhanced text further support the student during the reading process.

In addition to serving as wonderful picture books in schools, libraries, homes, and other places where children learn to love reading, these books are specifically intended to be read within an instructional guided reading group. This small group setting allows beginning readers to work with a fluent adult model as they make meaning from the text. After children develop fluency with the text and content, the book can be read independently. Children and adults alike will find these books supportive, engaging, and fun!

— Susan Nations, M.Ed., author, literacy coach,
and consultant in literacy development

Do you like to eat oatmeal for breakfast? Oatmeal is made out of oats. Oats are **cereal grains**.

Cereal grains are foods
that come from plants.
Wheat and rice are grains.
Popcorn is a grain, too!

7

Grains are part of the **food pyramid**. The six colored bands on the food pyramid stand for types of foods. Make smart choices. Eat these foods and **exercise** every day.

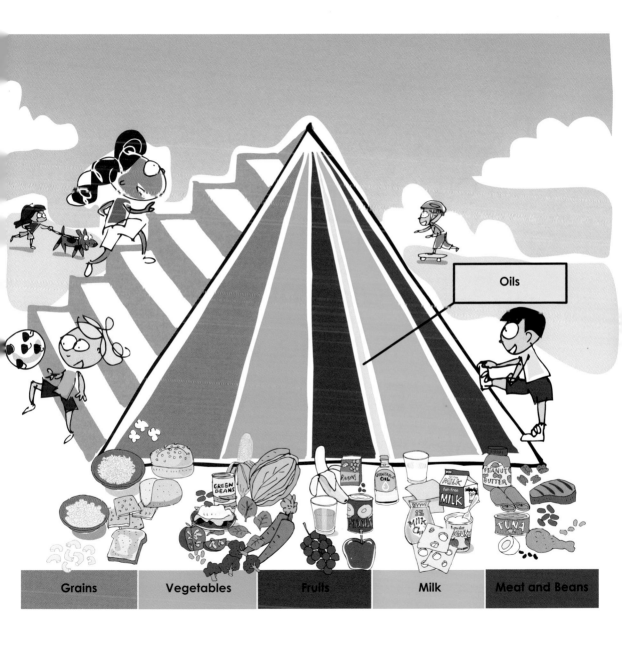

Oils

Grains Vegetables Fruits Milk Meat and Beans

The orange band stands for grains and foods made from grains. Bread and noodles are made from grains. It is the widest band. Every day, you should eat more grains than any other food group.

What other kinds of grains do you eat? Do you eat crackers, pretzels, or bread? All of these foods are made from grains.

13

Grains are good for you to eat. They help your heart stay **healthy**.

Grains build strong bones. They also help you run and play. Grains even help you go to the bathroom!

Some kinds of grains are better for you than others. **Whole grains** are the best. Bread made from whole wheat tastes good, too!

How can you eat enough whole grains? Pancakes can be made with whole wheat. You can even eat whole wheat muffins!

Glossary

food pyramid — the drawing that shows six colored bands that stand for the six different food groups people should eat every day

grains — cereal plants, such as wheat, corn, and oats

healthy — strong and free from illness

whole grains — the inside and the outside of grain kernels, or seeds

For More Information

Books

The Grain Group. Healthy Eating with MyPyramid (series). Mari C. Schuh (Capstone Press)

Grains. Blastoff! Readers: The New Food Guide Pyramid (series). Emily K. Green (Scholastic)

Grains. First Step Nonfiction (series). Robin Nelson (Lerner Publications)

Web Site

My Pyramid for Kids

mypyramid.gov/kids/index.html
Click on links to play a game and learn more at the government's Web site about the food pyramid.

Publisher's note to educators and parents: Our editors have carefully reviewed this Web site to ensure that it is suitable for children. Many Web sites change frequently, however, and we cannot guarantee that a site's future contents will continue to meet our high standards of quality and educational value. Be advised that children should be closely supervised whenever they access the Internet.

Index

About the Author

Tea Benduhn writes and edits books for children and teens. She lives in the beautiful state of Wisconsin with her husband and two cats. The walls of their home are lined with bookshelves filled with books. Tea says, "I read every day. It is more fun than watching television!"